Shh!
Can you
keep a secret?

You're about to meet the
Ballet Bunnies, who live hidden
at Millie's ballet school.

Are you ready?

Tiptoe this
way. . . .

Meet the Ballet Bunnies

Dolly

You'll never meet
a bunny who
loves to dance as
much as Dolly.

Fifi

If you're in
trouble, Fifi is
always ready to
lend a helping paw!

Pod

Pod loves to build things out of the bits and pieces he finds. He also loves his tutu!

Trixie

Yawn! When she's not dancing, Trixie likes curling up and having a nice snooze.

For Reuben

Text copyright © 2020 by Swapna Reddy
Cover art and interior illustrations copyright © 2020 by Binny Talib

All rights reserved. Published in the United States by Random House Children's Books, a division of Penguin Random House LLC, New York. Originally published in paperback by Oxford University Press, Oxford, in 2020.

Random House and the colophon are registered trademarks and A Stepping Stone Book and the colophon are trademarks of Penguin Random House LLC.

Visit us on the Web!
rhcbooks.com

Educators and librarians, for a variety of teaching tools, visit us at
RHTeachersLibrarians.com

Library of Congress Cataloging-in-Publication Data is available upon request.
ISBN 978-0-593-30495-2 (pbk.) — ISBN 978-0-593-30496-9 (lib. bdg.) —
ISBN 978-0-593-30497-6 (ebook)

MANUFACTURED IN CHINA
10 9 8 7 6 5 4 3 2 1
First American Edition 2021

This book has been officially leveled by using the
F&P Text Level Gradient™ Leveling System.

Ballet  Bunnies

Let's Dance

By Swapna Reddy

Illustrated by Binny Talib

A STEPPING STONE BOOK™
Random House 🏠 New York

Chapter 1

Miss Luisa's School of Dance was surprisingly noisy when Millie turned up for her ballet lesson. The usual buzz of students hurrying to lessons and the plinking of the piano in the nearby studio were drowned out today by overexcited dancers shouting to be heard.

Millie squeezed through the crowd gathered in the hallway and headed for the studio ahead of her classmates. She checked that no one had followed her before she

hurried inside and over to the curtained stage. She knew exactly who could tell her what was going on at Miss Luisa's School of Dance.

"Millie!" Fifi squealed. Millie clambered onto the stage and scooped up the tiny bunny hopping toward her.

The rest of the Ballet Bunnies—Dolly, Pod, and Trixie—were all sitting by an overturned teacup table, finishing their breakfast.

"What's going on?" Millie asked, turning and pointing at the crowded hallway.

"Isn't it thrilling?" Dolly cried. She pirouetted toward Millie. "There's going to be a gala performance!"

Millie looked confused. True, in front of her were four *talking* bunnies—well, *three* talking bunnies, to be accurate. Trixie had balled herself up and was lying under the soft fabric of a discarded tutu. She was snoring gently. But it wasn't the talking bunnies that confused Millie.

"What's a gala performance?" she asked.

"Dolly!" Pod said, pulling on his long ears. "I thought we weren't going to say anything until Millie heard the news from Miss Luisa."

"I don't care. I'm too excited!" Dolly danced in circles and then grabbed Pod's

paw and spun him toward Millie. "The gala performance is *only* the biggest ballet show of the year!" she exclaimed. "Everyone at Miss Luisa's School of Dance is involved!"

"Including you, Millie," Fifi said, nudging her, then jumping down to join Pod and Dolly.

A wide grin stretched across Millie's face. "I'll be dancing onstage?" she said. "In front of an audience—like a real ballet dancer?"

Fifi and Dolly nodded excitedly while Pod peered around the curtain at the studio.

"Millie, quick!" he whispered. "Your class is about to start!"

Chapter 2

"We're going to be in a show!" Samira screeched as soon as she spotted Millie.

"I know!" Millie shrieked back at her friend.

"How did you find out?" Samira said. "I was looking for you in the hallway when

Miss Luisa revealed the surprise, but I didn't see you."

"Oh, I heard it from a little bunny," Millie said, fiddling with the hem of her tutu.

"You are silly, Millie." Samira smiled and shook her head.

"Well, you haven't heard *everything*," their classmate Amber said smugly, joining the duo. "We're going to be dancing with props." She glared down her nose at Millie. "*I* know because *my* mom has arranged it all."

Before the girls could say anything else, Miss Luisa tapped the wooden barre, calling the class to attention.

"As I announced earlier," she said, "this year's performance will be *The Garden*."

Samira grabbed Millie's arm, and they grinned at each other.

"The oldest students will be our swans, the little kids will be the seedlings, and you will all be the flower fairies," Miss Luisa explained.

The entire class took a huge breath. Flower fairies! Amber even gave Millie an excited smile before remembering that they weren't friends. Then she dropped her beam to a frown.

"All of us, Miss Luisa?" she asked. "Some of us haven't been dancing as long as the others, and I'm worried they'll bring the performance down." She looked deliberately at Millie so that everyone knew exactly who she was talking about.

"Yes, Amber," Miss Luisa replied. "The whole class will be performing together, so you must work as a team."

Chapter 3

Miss Luisa pointed to a box in the corner of the studio.

"You will all take a watering can from the box. You cannot lose it, so please remember which is yours."

Everyone charged over to the box to pick their favorite colors. As Millie reached down for the blue can, Amber snatched it out of her hands.

"But you already have the pink one," Millie said, staring at the two watering cans in Amber's hands.

"Well, now I want the blue," snapped Amber, dropping the pink one so that it clattered on the wooden floor.

"Be careful with your props," Miss Luisa scolded. Millie picked up the abandoned watering can.

She hugged the pink watering can close to her chest and carried it over to the middle of the studio to join her class. Millie didn't mind all that much that it wasn't the blue can—she was too excited about the show. Not even Amber could bring her down today. Besides, pink was one of her favorite colors too.

"First, we will practice without the props," instructed Miss Luisa.

Everyone placed their watering cans off to the side. Then Miss Luisa talked the class through the ballet routine. Millie, who had

been dancing for a few weeks now, found herself picking up the steps quickly. She had a bunny or four to thank for the extra lessons she'd had.

But when the students picked up their

props, they all forgot their steps and soon found themselves in a knot of arms, legs, and cans. Even Will, the best dancer in the class, dropped his watering can a few times.

"It's a good thing there's no water in this," Samira said. She untangled her arms from Millie's and sent her prop crashing to the floor for the millionth time.

"Samira, please remember you are a flower fairy, not a frog," Miss Luisa said, straightening Samira's back. "I want to see graceful and light footwork."

Samira swung her watering can out and pirouetted straight into the barre. She collapsed in a heap on the floor before

pretending to take a long drink from the spout. Even Miss Luisa giggled.

"At least be a graceful frog," she said, laughing and pulling Samira to her feet.

By the end of the lesson, Millie was proud of herself and the rest of the class. They had worked hard together and looked like a real ballet troupe. Millie and Amber had even managed to steer clear of each other and avoid an argument.

As an end-of-class treat, Miss Luisa showed them their costumes for the show. The girls each had a tutu made up of fabric petals that matched the color of their watering can. The boys got to choose their tights and leotard sets, each embellished with flowers. Millie ran her hand over the velvet-soft petals on her pink tutu. She couldn't wait for the gala performance.

Chapter 4

Millie spent the entire week rehearsing as much as she could. She tottered around the house with her watering can. She practiced in the park. She spun around the dinner table. At bedtime, when her feet ached and she couldn't stifle the yawns, she made herself lift up her chin and stretch her

neck. She was determined to be the most graceful flower fairy at Miss Luisa's School of Dance.

On the day of the dress rehearsal, Millie made sure she was the first to arrive at the school. She wanted to pick up her costume early, but she also wanted to tell the Ballet Bunnies how hard she had been working on the routine.

"Please take us to the theater with you," Fifi said as Millie gathered her up with the rest of the bunnies in a ginormous hug. "We can come to the dress rehearsal, stay over, and be ready for the real performance!"

"Oh, bunny fluff! Please, Millie!" Dolly insisted. "Last time we traveled to the theater, we had to hide in the box of spare ballet slippers, and Trixie kept disappearing into the shoes."

"Will you be okay staying overnight at the theater?" Millie asked.

"Of course!" said Pod. "We wouldn't want to miss your big moment."

"We've packed our overnight bags," Trixie added.

There, stacked neatly in a row, were four tiny squares of silk that had been rolled up and pinned to make bunny-sized sleeping bags.

Millie opened her backpack, and Fifi, Dolly, Pod, and Trixie hopped in with their bags. Holding her costume, Millie carefully carried her friends to the bus, where Samira had saved a seat for her.

The theater was a short drive from the school. As the bus pulled up to the theater, Millie felt the bubble of excitement in her belly grow. Both she and Samira had been humming the flower fairies song the whole way, but they fell silent when the bus

stopped. There were grand columns at the entrance, paved marble tiles, and huge oak doors with twirly golden handles.

Miss Luisa got out first to pull open the theater doors. The children walked in pairs through the long red-carpeted lobby.

"Off you go," Millie whispered to the bunnies as she dropped to the floor, pretending to tie her shoelaces.

One by one, the bunnies snuck out of Millie's backpack and scampered behind the popcorn stand and out of sight.

Millie followed her classmates through the lobby and into the theater hall. Rows and rows of red velvet seats lined the hall—all the way from the front of the stage to the doors at the back of the room. As Millie looked up at the intricately painted ceiling, she could also see seats at different levels, reaching high up to the top.

On performance night, many of the seats would be filled. And each and every person in those seats would be watching Millie.

Chapter 5

The dancers climbed onstage and split off into their groups. The older students left to practice offstage, while Millie's class and the little kids were guided to the dressing rooms to try on their costumes.

Millie got ready quickly, then stood on the stage and looked out at the sea of chairs.

The excited bubble in her tummy was disappearing fast, and a swirl of knots was growing instead. When Miss Luisa called her class to rehearse, Millie's throat was dry and

her feet seemed frozen to the floor like solid ice blocks.

"What are you doing?" Amber hissed at her. "Miss Luisa has called us."

Millie opened her mouth to reply, but
the words did not come. As the flower fairies
song started to boom from the speakers,
Millie found herself forcing her legs to move
in time with her classmates—but she was
concentrating so hard on not dropping her
watering can that she was in plié when she
should have been in relevé, and in relevé
when she should have been in plié.

"Millie," Miss Luisa said
gently. "Why don't we take
a break and practice
offstage for a while?"

Millie nodded and
ran as fast as she could

away from the stage and the rows and rows
of seats.

Samira followed her. "Wait for me," she
whispered nervously behind Millie.

But before Millie could say a word, the rest of their class had joined them.

"You'd better not mess up like that on the night of our performance," Amber snarled. "You're

going to make us *all* look bad."

Millie frowned. Her stomach churned. She didn't want to make anyone look bad. What was she going to do?

Chapter 6

As the little kids took to the stage to rehearse their seedling routine, Millie changed out of her costume, found a quiet corner behind the curtains, and hid from her class.

She had rehearsed *all* week. She knew the routine by heart. She could probably perform it in her sleep! But when she looked out at the rows of seats and imagined them filled with hundreds of people, her feet refused to move.

"Millie?" a tiny voice called.

Millie looked down and recognized Dolly's familiar silky coat.

"Oh, Dolly," she said, relieved. "I'm so glad you're here."

"Come on," Dolly said. "I'll show you where we've set up camp."

Millie followed Dolly around the back of the stage toward a set of shelves. The bunnies had made themselves at home. A small thread of lights lit up a cozy shelf. On the shelf were two popcorn trays for beds. They were lined with soft silk and velvet from a discarded costume.

"Didn't Pod do well?" Fifi said as Millie peered in at their hideaway.

"He did," Millie said, smiling at the clever bunny.

On another shelf, Millie saw that the rest of the silk and velvet had been used to

create curtains, which had been tied back with gold ribbon from the tops of the candy bags that were sold in the lobby.

"What's this?" Millie asked.

Fifi pirouetted between the curtains and leapt high before landing in a curtsy. "This is *our* theater," she said with a bow. "We're putting on our own ballet show tonight for the theater mice, and they're going to perform a play for us!"

"That sounds cool!" Millie exclaimed. "I wish I could see it."

"Our gala performance is called *The Ballet Bunny Garden*, and we're all going to be Ballet Bunny flower fairies," Fifi explained.

"I'm going to be the pink one, just like you, Millie," Dolly added, holding up a pink cupcake liner that she had turned into a tutu.

Millie grinned, but her smile disappeared when Dolly asked about her rehearsal.

"I don't know what happened," she said sadly. "I rehearsed nonstop all week, but everything went wrong today. I'm so worried about making a mistake that it's making me make lots of mistakes!"

"Oh, Millie, you're nervous about performing onstage," Fifi said gently.

"I understand, Millie," Dolly said. "I feel the same way about dancing for the mice. I'm worried I'll forget my steps too."

"But you're so good, Dolly!" Millie said. "You have nothing to be nervous about. You always look like you are having so much fun when you're dancing. Even if you *do* make a mistake, no one will notice because they'll be having so much fun with you."

Dolly smiled at Millie. "You're right," she said slowly. "I can only do my best. I should just try and enjoy it and stop worrying."

"Exactly," Fifi agreed, nodding along. Then she, Dolly, and Pod smiled up at Millie.

Millie smiled back. Even if *she* made a small mistake, everyone would see how much she loved dancing too.

Why hadn't she told herself that earlier?

Chapter 7

"Are you ready, Millie?" Trixie asked, joining Dolly and Fifi.

"I think so." Millie picked up Trixie and nuzzled the bunny's fur against her cheek.

"When I'm nervous, I take some deep breaths in and out. It helps me calm down," Trixie said. "I can show you if you want."

"Yes please," Millie replied.

She sat on the floor. Trixie and the other three bunnies joined her.

"Shut your eyes," Trixie told them.

Millie and the bunnies closed their eyes obediently.

"Now breathe in," Trixie said.

They all inhaled.

"And breathe out," she said, nodding as they exhaled their deep breaths.

"In."

"Out."

"In."

"Out."

"Zzzzzzzz."

Millie opened her eyes to find that Trixie's calming breaths had put the tiniest of the bunnies right to sleep. Pod giggled,

and Fifi had to put a paw over Pod's mouth to stop him from waking Trixie. Millie picked Trixie up and gently placed her in a popcorn-tray bed.

"Bunny fluff!" Fifi exclaimed. "I've just had an idea!"

She hopped toward Millie's watering can and jumped in.

Millie peered in, and the little bunny peered back up, her eyes shiny with excitement.

"Dolly could be inside your watering can while you dance, and that way you won't be alone," Fifi said. "She'll remind you to have fun!" The little bunny spun a pirouette inside the can. "Pod could make a seat from some of the old programs, and it will be just like a ride at the fair."

Dolly leapt up and down as she and Millie squealed with glee at the idea of being onstage together in the show.

Chapter 8

Performance night arrived.
Miss Luisa was wandering around backstage,
checking costumes and props, while the
students slipped on their ballet shoes and
talked through their routines. The noise in
the theater hall was building as families and
friends filled the rows and rows of seats.

Millie smoothed down the petals of her tutu and patted her hair, which Mom had pulled up into a neat bun high on her head. Mom had even added some sparkles to Millie's cheeks before wishing her luck and heading into the hall to find a front-row seat.

"Please leave your props at the side of the stage," Miss Luisa called out. "And good luck, everyone," she said, giving them all a huge thumbs-up.

Millie squinted to look inside her watering can. Dolly was strapped in tight to a padded seat that Pod had made from some old programs and a ticket book.

"Are you okay in there?" Millie asked.

"Yes." Dolly looked up with a big grin. "Are you okay out there?"

Millie tried to nod, but her tummy felt like it had a swarm of butterflies inside it, trying hard to escape.

"Let's all try Trixie's calming breaths," Dolly said.

They breathed in and out and in and out. With every breath, Millie felt the churning feeling in her tummy lessen, as though she were blowing out the butterflies with each lungful.

Millie gave Dolly a tiny kiss on the head before placing the watering can down with the other props. She took her place next to Samira. Then the curtains came apart.

The performance was about to begin.

Chapter 9

"Flower fairies," Miss Luisa whispered to the children. "You're up next!"

Millie tore her eyes away from the older students, who were halfway through their swan dance. She rushed toward the props to find her watering can and Dolly.

"Good luck, Millie," Samira said as she

hurried past with her own can. "See you up there!"

"Good luck, Samira," Millie whispered back excitedly.

She reached the side of the stage and looked for her pink can. It wasn't there. It wasn't where she'd left it. She checked behind the curtain, under the table, and in the boxes. She searched the backpacks and the lunch boxes. Her watering can had completely disappeared.

"Oh no. Oh no. Oh no," she whispered, panicked.

"What's wrong, Millie?" Fifi asked, hopping over with Pod and Trixie. "We just came to wish you and Dolly good luck."

"My watering can is gone!" Millie said, hunting through the folds of the curtain again. "And Dolly's inside."

Her hands shook as she shoved her way through boxes of costumes, dumping them onto their sides, searching for the little bunny.

Millie suddenly stopped. There on the floor where her watering can had been was a blue petal. A blue petal from a blue flower tutu.

"Amber!" Millie cried. "Amber took the can, and Dolly too."

"Don't worry, Millie," Fifi reassured her. "Dolly's made of tough bunny fluff. We'll find her."

Catching Dolly's scent, the bunnies dashed off behind the stage. Millie sprinted after them.

"She's here somewhere!" Pod said, his long ears twitching. "I can hear her!"

"I can't hear anything," Millie said as the swan song blared loudly backstage.

"She's definitely here," Pod said. "I can hear her thumping her feet."

"In here!" Fifi shouted, jumping up and down by a closed trash can. "I think Dolly's in here."

Millie yanked off the lid. There, inside the dark bin, was her pink watering can and an agitated—but safe—Dolly.

Millie lifted Dolly out of the watering can and hugged her close. "Are you okay?" she asked.

"I'm fine," Dolly huffed. "That Amber took our can and dumped it in the trash."

"I thought so," replied Millie, before telling her about the blue petal.

"I could have climbed out, but the lid was too heavy," Dolly said. "Thankfully, Amber didn't see me."

The last few lines of the swan song played. There were only a few seconds left before Millie had to be onstage.

"I think we have a show to do," Dolly said, hearing the music die down.

She jumped out of Millie's hands and back into the watering can.

"Are you sure?" Millie asked.

"Yes!" Dolly grinned. "Not even Amber can ruin our fun tonight."

Chapter 10

"There you are!" Samira said as Millie skidded to a stop by her friend. "We're on!"

The music for their performance began, and the flower fairies took to the stage. A feeling of calm came over Millie when she spotted Mom, whooping for her louder than anyone else in the audience.

Millie felt her body rock and sway to the music as she bobbed up and down in time with the others. She had been so busy trying to find Dolly backstage that she hadn't had time to feel nervous.

Dolly cheered Millie on the whole way through the performance. And not once did Millie feel nervous! When the song ended, she just wanted it to start all over again so she could dance some more.

The crowd was on their feet as Millie and her class curtsied and bowed. The sea of seats was now an ocean of smiles. Samira grabbed Millie's hand, and she and Millie

took another curtsy as the crowd cheered even louder. Out of the corner of her eye, Millie spotted Amber stomping off the stage.

Millie stuck out her chin and thrust her shoulders back before taking a final curtsy. As she lowered her head, she spotted Dolly beaming up at her with pride.

"You did it!" the little bunny whispered. Millie's heart felt so full. She couldn't wait for the gala performance next year.

Basic ballet moves

First position

Second position

Third
position

Fourth
position

Fifth position

Glossary of ballet terms

Arabesque—Standing on one leg, the
   dancer extends the other leg
   out behind them.

Barre—A horizontal bar at
   waist level on which ballet
   dancers rest a hand for
   support during certain
   exercises.

Demi-plié—A small bend of
   the knees, with heels kept on the floor.

En pointe—Dancing on the very tips of the
   toes.

Grand plié—A large bend of the knees,
   with heels raised off the floor.

Pas de deux—A dance for two people.

Pirouette—A spin made on one foot, turning all the way around.

Plié—A movement in which the dancer bends the knees and straightens them again while feet are turned out and heels are kept on the floor.

Relevé—A movement in which the dancer rises on the tips of the toes.

Sauté—A jump off both feet, landing in the same position.

Twirl and spin with
the Ballet Bunnies
in their next adventure!

Turn the page for a sneak peek.

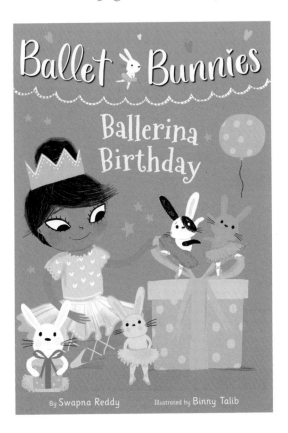

Chapter 2

Taking the bunnies home in her bag was going to be tricky. They were far too heavy for Millie to be able to skip all the way home the way she usually did with Mom. And if she didn't skip, Mom might start asking questions.

So Millie kept Trixie tucked up away in

her pocket, while Dolly snuck into Millie's bag.

"We can follow behind and keep out of sight," Pod and Fifi had agreed.

Millie kept Mom as distracted as possible on the way home, asking her questions about her day and sharing stories from the last ballet class.

Just a few doors away from their house, Mom stopped suddenly and spun around to look behind Millie, who turned to see that Fifi and Pod must have darted behind a nearby tree trunk to stand as still as statues.

"Mom?" Millie started. She bounced

nervously from foot to foot and held on to Trixie a little tighter.

Mom shook her head and turned back. "I thought someone was behind us," she said, confused, before skipping on beside Millie all the way to their front door.

⊙ ✳ ⊙

"That was close!" Dolly said as she scrambled out of Millie's bag the moment the four bunnies were safely in Millie's bedroom.

Pod picked out a leaf from his fur. "I told you we should have hidden behind that mailbox, Fifi."

"Oh, bunny fluff," Fifi said, dismissively. "We're all here now, aren't we?"

She bounced up
and down on Millie's
bed, before lying back
in the soft sheets. "This
is going to be the best
bunny vacation ever,"
she said, grinning at
the others.

Trixie yawned,
and her nose twitched
as Millie placed her

carefully down by her musical jewelry box. The little bunny popped open the lid to see the tiny ballerina inside begin to rotate to the tune from the box. Fifi, Pod, and Dolly giggled with glee, and together all four bunnies pirouetted around the box in time with the twinkly melody.

Discover more magic in these page-turning adventures!

For the totally
unique ballerina!

For the
unicorn-obsessed!

For dog lovers
and budding pirates!

For cat lovers and
wannabe mermaids!